ESTHER

Told and Illustrated by

LISL WEIL

ATHENEUM   1980   NEW YORK

Remembering my husband

LIBRARY OF CONGRESS CATALOGING IN PUBLICATION DATA

Weil, Lisl.   Esther.

SUMMARY: A retelling of the Old Testament story
of the young Jewish girl
who became queen of Persia and used her influence
to stop the murder of the Jews living in exile
in Persia.
1. Esther, Queen of Persia—Juvenile literature.
2. Bible. O. T.—Biography—Juvenile literature.
[1. Esther, Queen of Persia. 2. Bible stories—O. T.]
I. Title.
BS580.E8W44   221'.92'4 [B] [92]   79-22543
ISBN 0-689-30761-6

Published simultaneously in Canada by
McClelland & Stewart, Ltd.
Printed by The Connecticut Printers, Inc.
Hartford, Connecticut
Bound by A. Horowitz & Sons/Bookbinders,
Fairfield, New Jersey
First Edition

This is the true story of
a beautiful girl,

a mighty king,

the foster-father of
the beautiful girl,

and an evil man.

Once in long ago Persia there lived a king named Ahasuerus. He ruled over one hundred and twenty-seven lands, from India to Ethiopia. And everywhere he ruled his word was law. Everyone had to do what he commanded.

Now it happened that one day he commanded his wife Vashti to do something that she said she would not do.

When he heard that she would not do as he asked, he was very angry, and he decided that Vashti should no longer be the queen. He made up his mind that he would never see her again.

But a King must have a queen, and Ahasuerus did not know where he would find one as beautiful as Vashti.

"Great King Ahasuerus," said one of his advisors finally, "we will search every corner of your kingdom. For you must have all the most beautiful girls in the land sent to your palace. Then you can take your choice."

This sounded good to Ahasuerus.

So the search began at once. Many beautiful girls from all parts of the kingdom were brought to the royal palace. All of them were given special baths and rubbed with fine oils to make them even more beautiful.

One of the girls who came was Esther. She had lived near the palace with her cousin Mordecai, who had adopted her when her parents died. Although no one in the palace knew it, Esther was not Persian but Hebrew. She and Mordecai were among the many Hebrews who lived in Persia because the Persians had conquered them and brought them here years before. Esther was beautiful, gentle and wise and soon made friends in the palace.

King Ahasuerus spent more than a year seeing all the lovely girls who had come hoping to be queen. At last he made his choice.

That choice was Esther.

Once he had made up his mind, the king gave a great banquet to honor Esther as his new queen. Esther was pleased. But, following the advice of Mordecai, she still did not tell anyone that she was a Hebrew.

Mordecai had come often to the gate of the palace to ask about Esther. But he had told no one that he was her foster-father.

Then just after Esther was made queen, he happened to hear two palace guards plotting to kill Ahasuerus.

Mordecai sent word
of this to Esther
at once.

And Esther immediately warned the king, telling him that it was a man named Mordecai who had discovered the plot. The guards were punished, and Mordecai's name was written down as the person who had saved the king.

Some years later, the king made a man named Haman his chief advisor. Haman was very vain, and he insisted that everyone in the city of Susa, around the king's palace, bow down to him. Everyone did but Mordecai. Because he was a Hebrew, he did not believe in bowing down to a man like Haman.

Haman was so angry, he decided he wanted to kill not only Mordecai, but all of the Hebrews.

He went to King Ahasuerus and said, "There are certain peoples in your land who are different from all others. They do not keep your royal laws, but follow their own ways. It is not good that they should be allowed to live. I will pay into your treasury ten thousand silver coins if you will allow me to kill these lawbreakers."

The king agreed to Haman's plan. And immediately word was sent out by Haman, in the king's name, that on a certain day all of the Hebrews in the king's lands were to be killed and their possessions were to be taken by others.

The Hebrews everywhere began to weep and mourn, Mordecai most of all, because he believed that the coming disaster was his fault.

Yet he also hoped that something might be done to save the people. After all, Esther was the queen. So as soon as he could, he sent word to her of what had happened.

"Perhaps it is for a time like this that I have been made the queen," Esther said to herself.

And even though it was against the law for her to go to the room where the king sat upon his throne, she went. The king forgave her for coming, because he loved her, and asked her what she wanted. She said simply that she wanted him to come, with Haman, to a special dinner she was preparing. The king and Haman were both delighted to be asked.

Before the day of the dinner, however, Haman saw Mordecai again and was so filled with hate that he decided to kill Mordecai even before the rest of the Hebrews were killed.

Haman had a great wooden gallows built on which to hang the man who would not bow down to him.

In the meantime, the king was reading over some of his old records and found the note about the murder plot and about Mordecai, the man who had saved him.

The king called in Haman and asked him what should be done to honor a man who had performed a great service. Haman, thinking the king meant him, said the man should be clothed in royal robes and led through the streets of the city on a royal horse with a royal crown upon his head. Furthermore, someone should go before the man announcing that this was someone the king had chosen to honor.

"Go at once and do this for Mordecai," said the king.

And Haman had to do it, though it made him very angry.

Afterward he went home feeling most unhappy. For the first time he wondered if his plans would really work out as he had hoped.

That night was the time set for Esther's dinner. And so, vain Haman consoled himself quickly, gloating over his invitation and dressing for dinner with great care.

The king and Haman arrived to a great feast of food and wine. When the meal was over, the king was so pleased he said to Esther, "Whatever you ask of me, I will give you."

In a voice filled with sadness and dignity, Esther answered at once. She said, "My request is that you spare my people and me. For we have been sold. I and all of my people, the Hebrews, are to be killed."

"And who is going to do such a thing as this?" asked the king, who had paid little attention to Haman's plans. "An enemy to me and my people," Esther answered. "This wicked Haman."

The king was so angry he walked out into the garden to try to decide what he should do.

Haman stayed behind to plead with Esther for his life. But it was of no use. The king returned, and learning that Haman had prepared a gallows for Mordecai, he ordered that Haman be hung from it.

Haman was hung as the king had ordered, and all of his possessions were given to Esther.

As for the law that all the Hebrews were to be killed, that could not be changed, for the king's laws could not be set aside.

But the king decreed that the Hebrew people had the right to defend themselves against any who might come to kill them. And he had his messengers proclaim it everywhere.

After Haman died, Queen Esther told the king that Mordecai was her foster-father. King Ahasuerus sent for him with joy, and in a great ceremony gave him all the honor and the power that had once been Haman's. Mordecai left the king's presence in royal robes, wearing a great crown and a cloak of fine linen. The whole city of Susa shouted for joy. And that night there was feasting in every Hebrew home.

When the day came on which the Hebrews were supposed to have been killed, it was their enemies who died instead. Once again there was great

feasting among the Hebrews, and Queen Esther asked that there be feasting every year at that time.

And just as Queen Esther had asked, it was done, forever after, in all of the one hundred and twenty-seven lands ruled by King Ahasuerus. The time that might have been a time of death became a time of laughter.

And still, today, Hebrew people everywhere celebrate what is called the feast of Purim and remember the wise and brave Queen Esther who saved her people. For the children it is a time for playing

and of merrymaking, and of eating a special cookie called Haman's Taschen.